THIS BOOK BELONGS TO

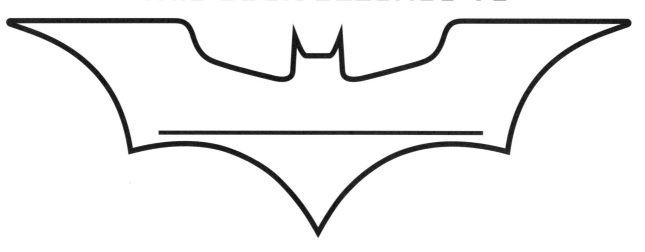

HarperFestival is an imprint of HarperCollins Publishers.

The Dark Knight Rises: Design and Draw Coloring and Activity Book
Copyright © 2012 DC Comics.
BATMAN and all related characters and elements
are trademarks of and © DC Comics.
(s12)

HARP5002

Printed in the United States of America.
No part of this book may be used or reproduced in any manner whatsoever without
written permission except in the case of brief quotations embodied in critical articles and reviews.
For information address HarperCollins Children's Books, a division of HarperCollins Publishers,
10 East 53rd Street, New York, NY 10022.
www.harpercollinschildrens.com
ISBN 978-0-06-213226-0
Book design by John Sazaklis
12 13 14 15 16 LP/BR 10 9 8 7 6 5 4 3 2 1
❖
First Edition

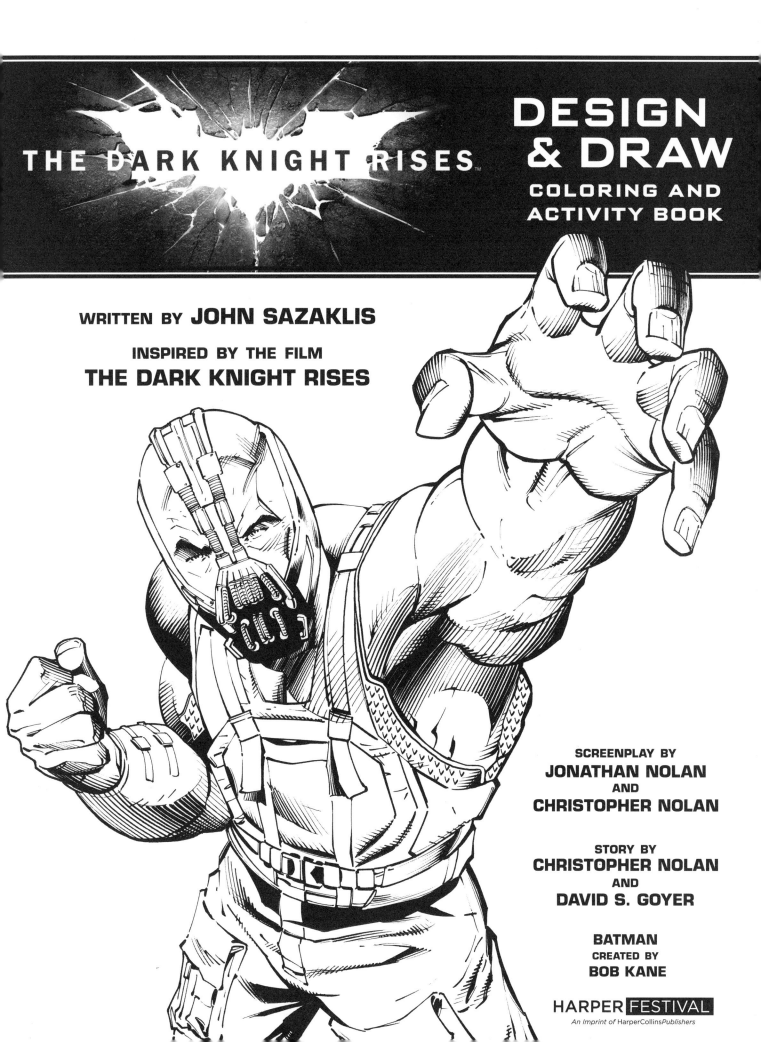

MEET BATMAN
He is the World's Greatest Detective.

ON PATROL

Batman fights crime in Gotham City.
Draw and color the city skyline.

Don't forget the Bat-Signal calling the hero to action!

WELCOME TO GOTHAM CITY
Batman swings over the skyscrapers using his cape and grappling hook.

Draw the hero in flight!

TO THE BATCAVE!
Batman's secret lair has everything he needs to fight crime.

What does your hideout look like? Draw it here!

TOOLS OF THE TRADE

The Dark Knight's arsenal is an array of advanced technology. Color in Batman's tools.

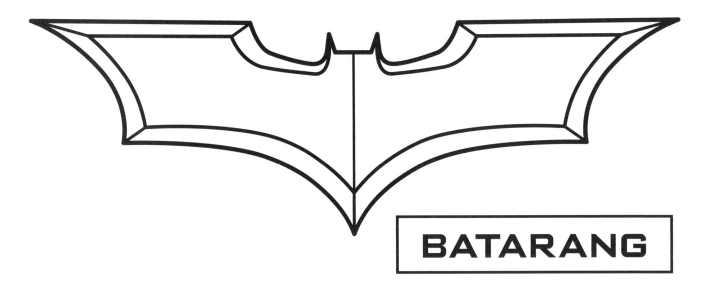

BATARANG

CELL PHONE

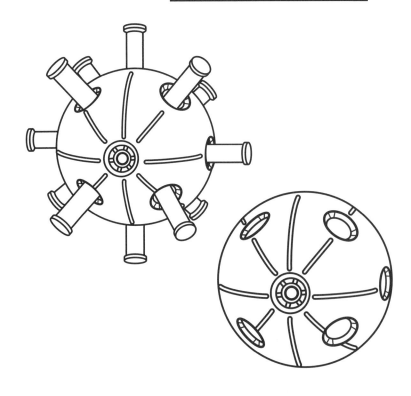

SMOKE BOMBS

GRAPNEL GUN

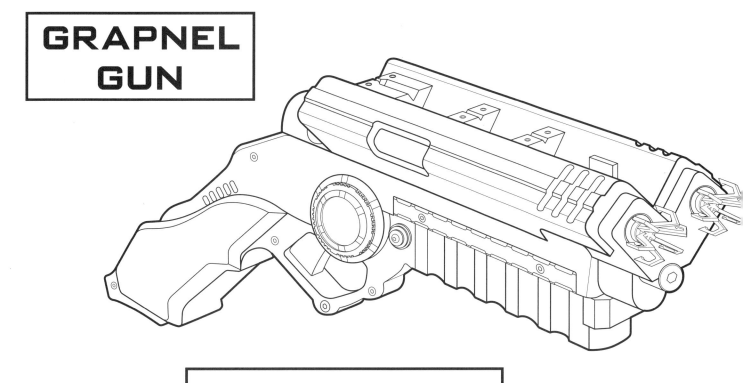

UTILITY BELT

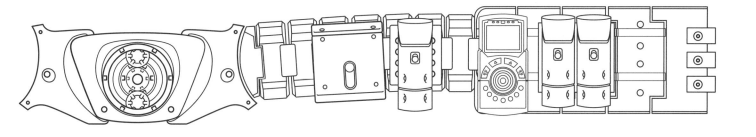

GAUNTLET

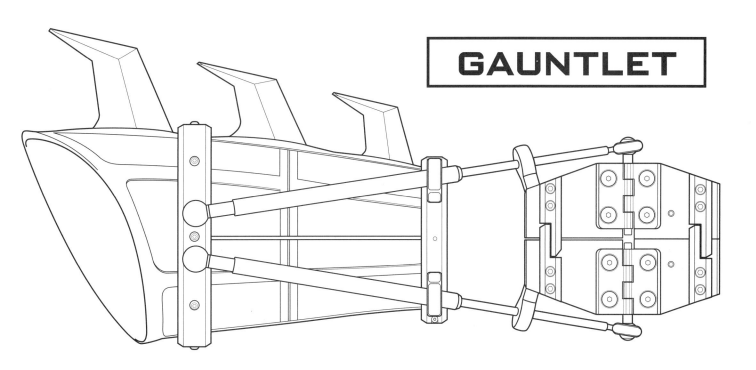

CRIME-FIGHTING ACCESSORIES

This is Batman's Utility Belt.
He keeps lots of tools and gadgets in it!

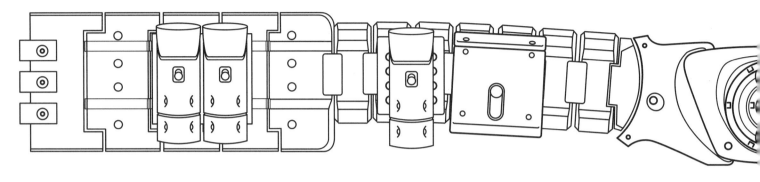

Draw your own Utility Belt and create your own gadgets. What do your tools do?

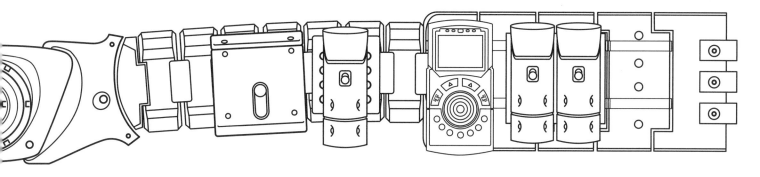

DRAW YOUR OWN BATARANG

Use the grid to make a copy of Batman's trusty weapon.

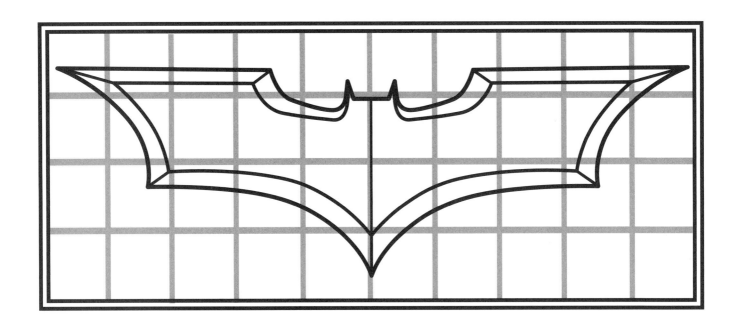

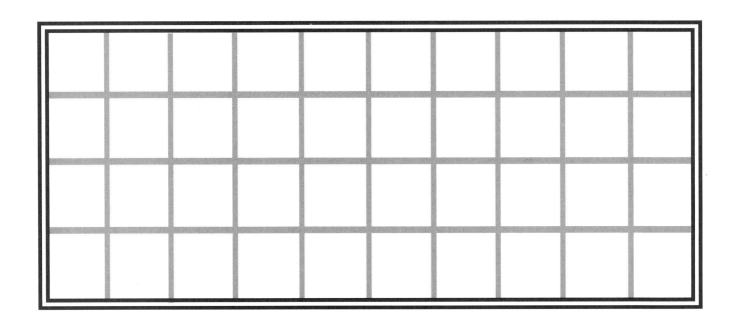

TARGET PRACTICE

Batman throws his Batarangs with perfect aim.
What other weapons can he throw?
Draw them in the space below.

AMAZING ARMOR

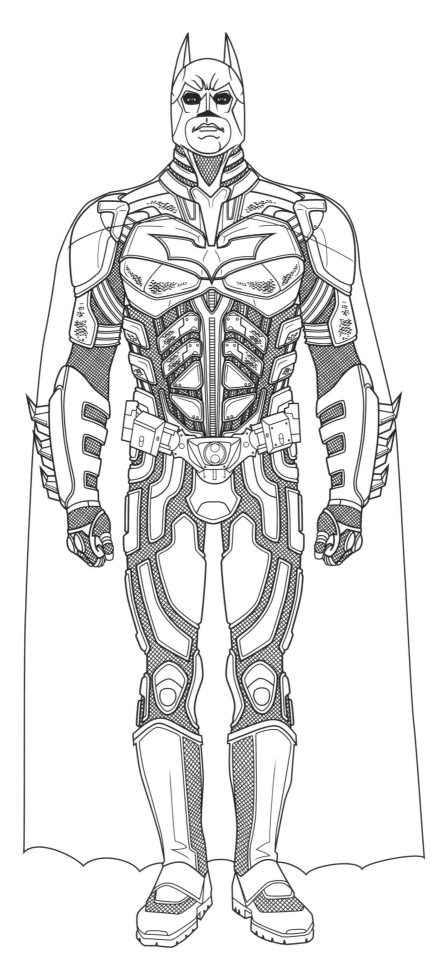

Batman's high-tech suit protects his body when he fights crime. Color it in.

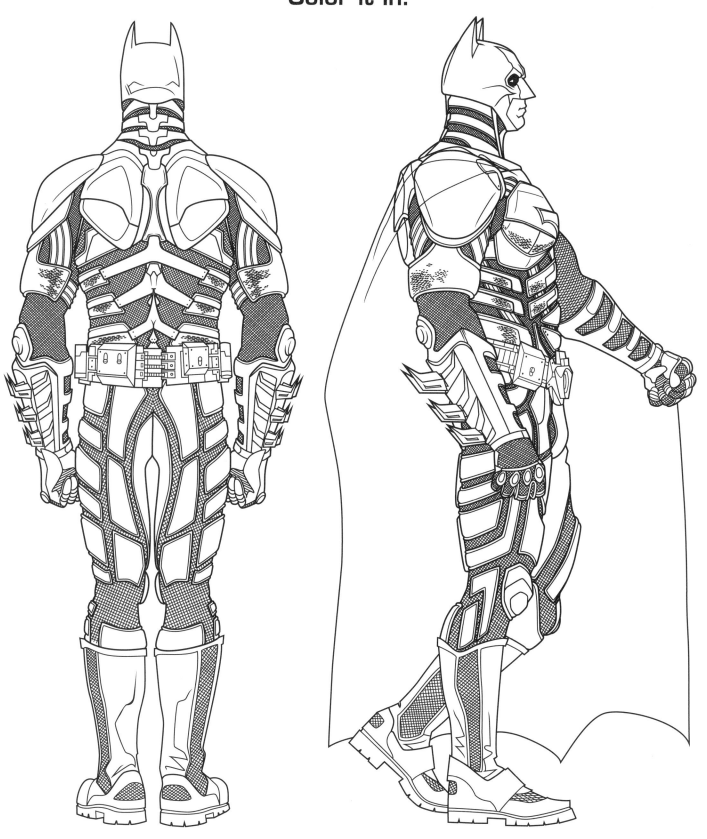

SUIT UP

Draw your own crime-fighting costume.

HEADGEAR

Does your costume have a helmet or mask?
Draw it here.

TO THE BATMOBILE!
This mighty mode of transportation allows Batman to ride over tough terrain.

THE BAT-POD
This lean, mean riding machine lets Batman navigate through tight spaces.

PARTY AT WAYNE MANOR

Bruce Wayne is having a party at his mansion.
Draw the ballroom full of decorations and guests.

Make sure to include your friends!

ON THE PROWL

One of the maids sneaks away from the party.
She's really Catwoman in disguise!
Draw her in action!

CATCH THE THIEF!

A priceless pearl necklace has been stolen from Wayne Manor. No time to waste. Batman is on the case!

EXTRA! EXTRA!

Another crime wave hits Gotham City, and you're covering the story. Finish your newspaper article in time for the morning edition!

Story by

PUBLIC ENEMY
What does Catwoman look like?
Draw your police sketch here.

WANTED

**BREAKING AND ENTERING
THEFT**
IF YOU HAVE ANY INFORMATION,
PLEASE CONTACT
THE GOTHAM CITY POLICE DEPARTMENT.

SECRETS REVEALED

Batman has discovered who Catwoman is!
Use the key below to decipher the code.

C	A	T	W	O	M	A	N
X	Z	G	D	L	N	Z	M

I	S		R	E	A	L	L	Y
R	H		I	V	Z	O	O	B

S	E	L	I	N	A		K	Y	L	E!
H	V	O	R	M	Z		P	B	O	V!

ANSWER KEY ON PAGE 64.

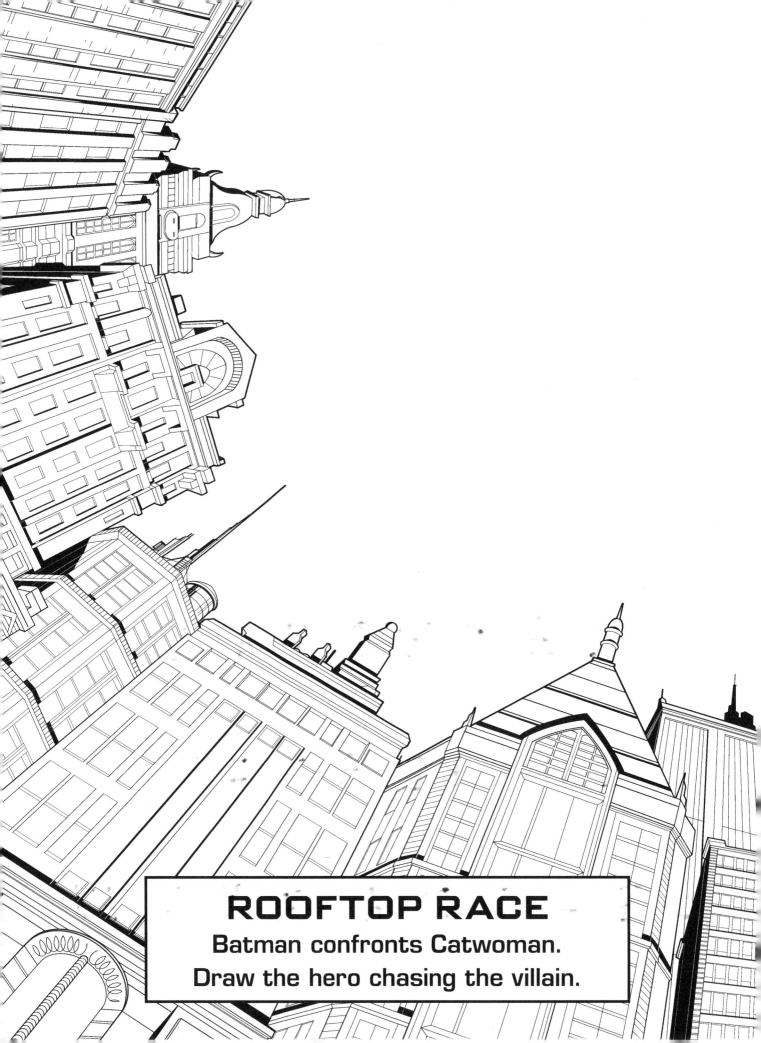

BATMAN VERSUS CATWOMAN

The Dark Knight has the criminal cornered. What happens next? Make up a story and draw the rest of the scene in the panels provided. Include word balloons and sound effects.

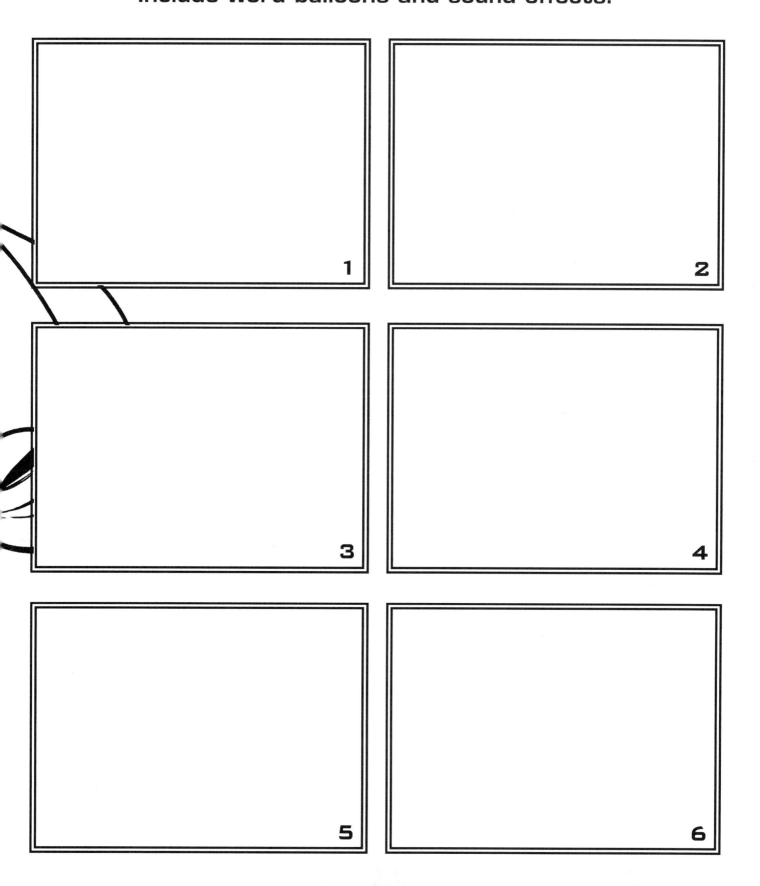

MASKED MENACE

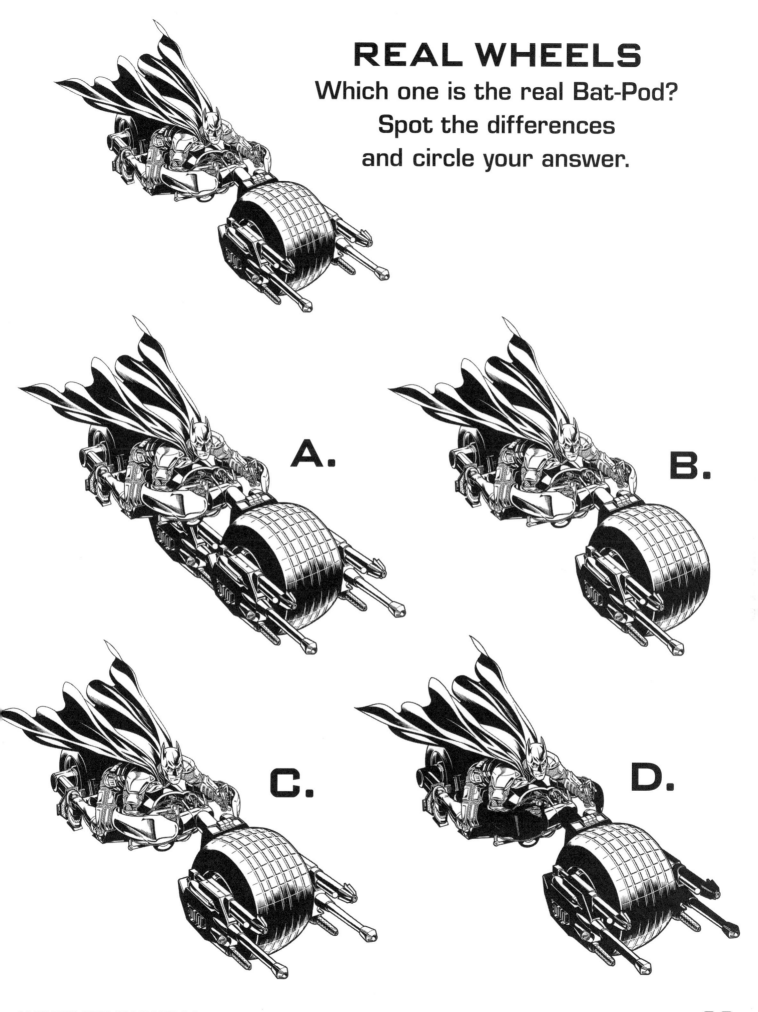

THIS JUST IN!
The Batcomputer alerts Batman to some breaking news.

WARNING

TROUBLE AT THE GOTHAM CITY STOCK EXCHANGE. CRIMINALS ARE ON THE LOOSE!

I AM BANE!
Batman's newest foe is a big, brawny bruiser.

SPEED DEMON
Draw Batman in one of his vehicles zooming to the rescue!

CRIMINAL CLUES

Bane has escaped but he left behind some evidence. Batman knows exactly where to look for his newest foe. Do you? Write your answer in the space below.

ANSWER KEY ON PAGE 64.

SECRET COMMUNICATION

Batman sends a text message to Commissioner Gordon. Trace over the dotted lines to reveal Batman's discovery.

CAPED CRUSADER
Batman is determined to bring Bane to justice.

BRUTE FORCE
Bane is determined to bring Batman down.

SEWER SEARCH

Find the words below within this puzzle.
They are hidden horizontally, vertically, and diagonally.
One is circled for you.

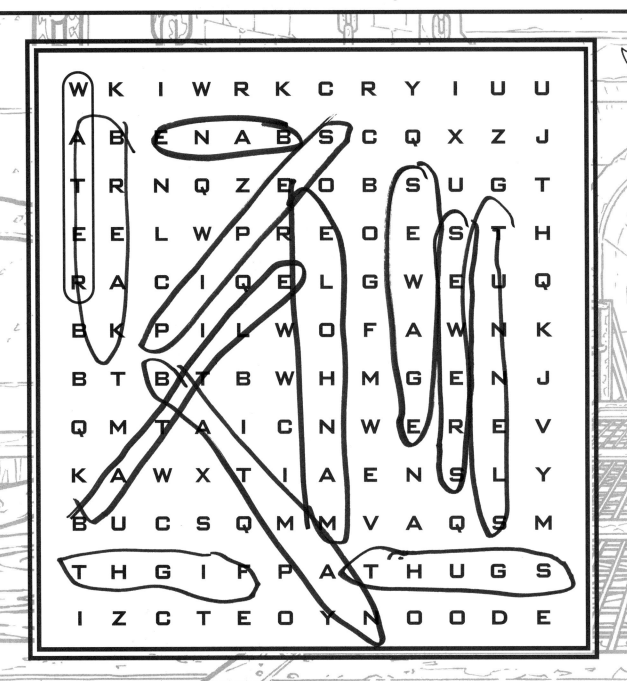

List of words:
BANE, BATMAN, BATTLE, BREAK,
FIGHT, MANHOLE, PIPES, SEWAGE,
SEWERS, THUGS, TUNNELS, WATER.

ANSWER KEY ON PAGE 64.

BATMAN VERSUS BANE

The Dark Knight battles his new nemesis.
Make up a story and draw the action in the panels provided.
Include word balloons and sound effects.

WATCH YOUR BACK!
Which one is the real Bane?
Spot the differences and circle your answer.

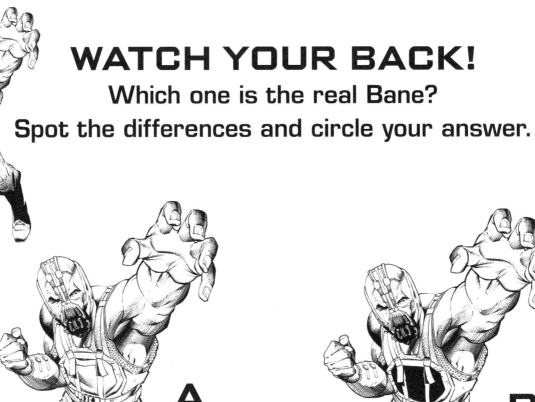
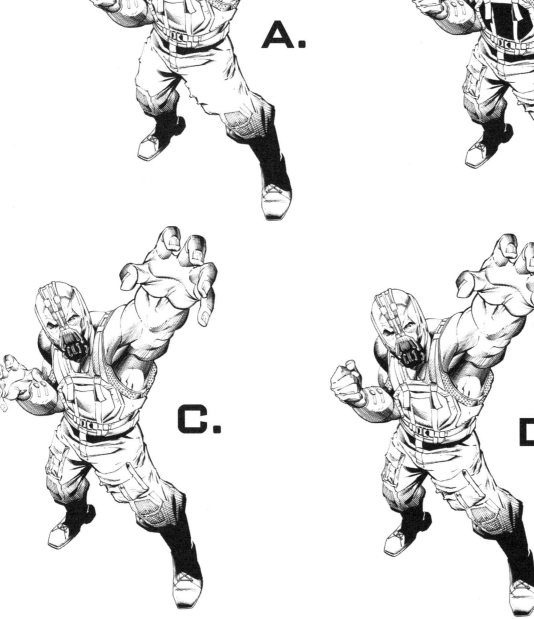

ANSWER KEY ON PAGE 64.

MONSTER MACHINE
Bane charges through the streets of Gotham in his own tank of terror!

YOU'RE HIRED!
Lucius Fox helps create Batman's vehicles.
He has a job for you.

WAYNE ENTERPRISES

APPLIED SCIENCES DIVISION

Dear Colleague,   **CONFIDENTIAL**

You have been commissioned to create a flying vehicle for Batman. This is the prototype:

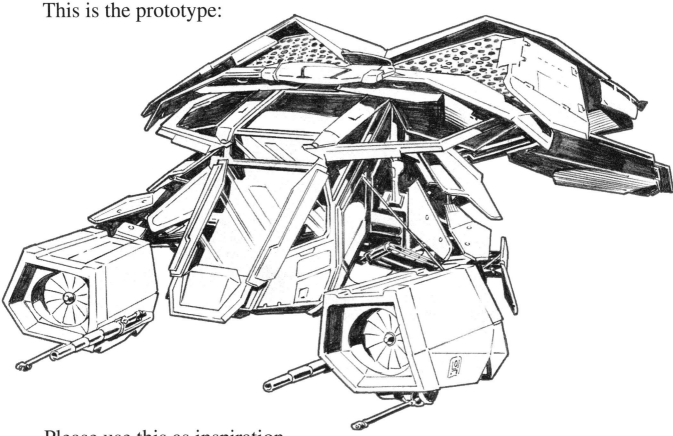

Please use this as inspiration.
We look forward to seeing your new and improved invention.

Sincerely,

Lucius Fox

Lucius Fox
Head of Wayne Enterprises

Create your flying vehicle here.

WAYNE ENTERPRISES
APPLIED SCIENCES DIVISION

TOP SECRET

BATMAN'S OTHER HALF
Use the grid and finish drawing the Dark Knight.

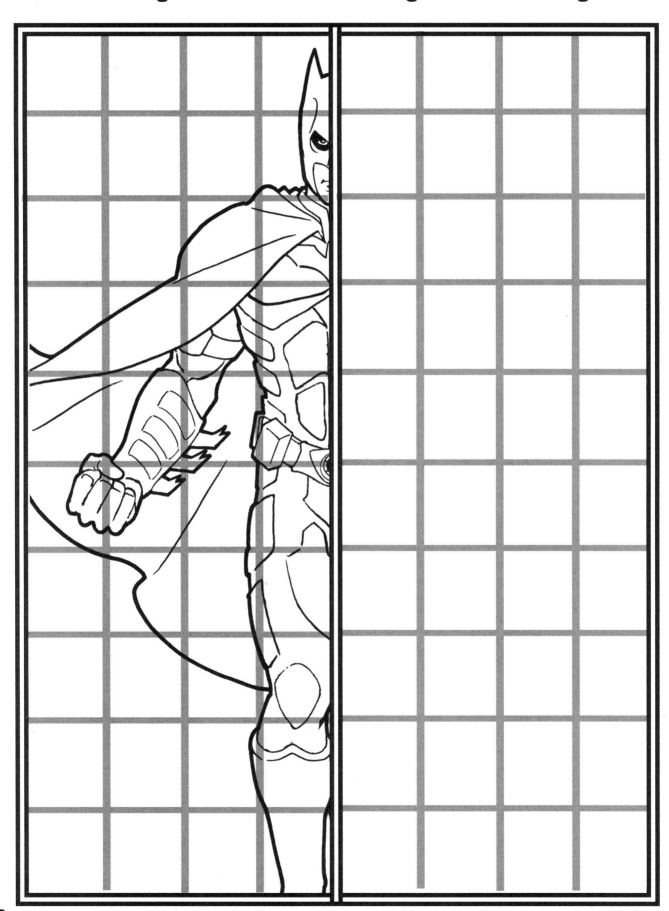

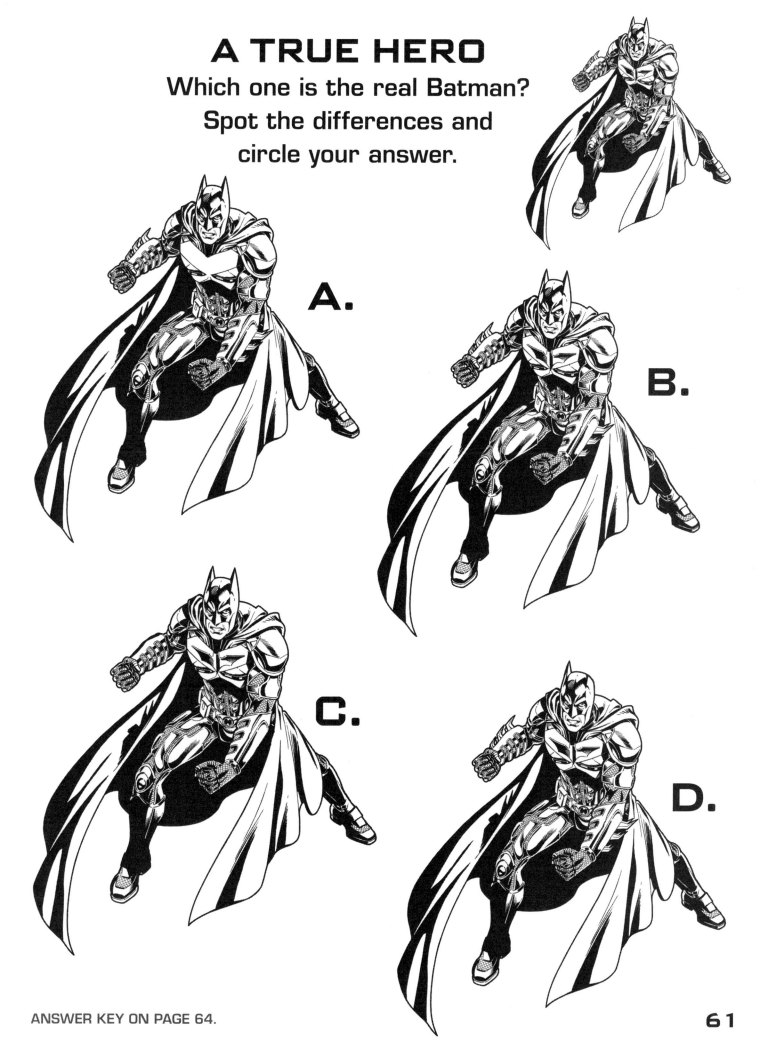

GOTHAM CITY GUARDIAN
For now, the city is at peace.
Draw Batman keeping a watchful eye on the streets.

ANSWER KEY

Page 33: Catwoman is really Selina Kyle!

Page 39: C

Page 44: The sewers.

Page 45: Bane is hiding in the sewers.

Page 48:

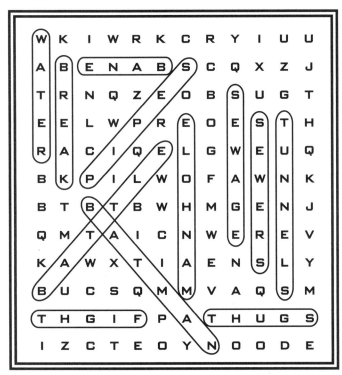

Page 49:

Page 54: D

Page 61: B